Once is Not Enough

Stories on love, passion, desire, family and loss

Geeta Lal Sahai

Heart & Soul Media

To all those unsung superheroes for helping us stay safe in the present day global crises – COVID 19.

Thank you for being there.

Contents

Once is Not Enough

Stories on love, passion,
desire, family and loss

Geeta Lal Sahai

Author's Note

These five short stories are about love, unrequited love, madness, delusion, loss, loneliness and dilemma. The settings for these short stories are Delhi, Mumbai, Uttar Pradesh, Haryana, Uttarakhand in India, not necessarily in that order. The characters and incidents can be placed in any other city. The protagonists have weaknesses but are trying to cling to life-support medicine – hope.

There is a first-person narrative, third person, and also a *sutradhar* (narrator) within the story's structure as we often see in plays. The overall storytelling style is confessional.

A word about the stories – the story –*Once Is Not Enough* is about an unrequited love; *The Singer* is about the frustration of a woman singer who has passed her heydays and is caught in a dead relationship; *The Birthday Cake*'s protagonist is a little boy and his world-view during the present-day global crises; *Lonely Footsteps* is about love, family secrets and tragedy and *My Father* is about the complex issue of caste, politics, mental health and love.

I always take inspiration from reality and real-life experiences, and while weaving a tale, I go beyond what is visible and add a slight twist. Some of these stories were written nearly five years ago.

I hope you like the collection, the varied themes and the unexpected, unpredicted journey of the characters in these stories.

Happy reading!

Geeta La Sahai

June 2021

Once is Not Enough

My Peacock's train had burnt out. The flame that was once there, the connection and intimacy, had dried out. It was now cold and miserable. I couldn't remember the last time I was happy. The last time I looked at his face and be proud of myself, proud of my life, I couldn't remember. I couldn't place myself in such happy, warm, unforgettable times. I was lost in the dark. While I stood there wondering at what point did my life take this awful turn, I stared at the Kumaon hills. The view was serene as it had been for the last fifteen years of my marriage. The slopes were painted green, but the blend was so satisfying with the morning fog because, in my head, the hills were given a white ice cap. I loved it, and each new day, I would stand by the window with my favourite woollen sweater on; and stare. But today, I had walked out of my cottage and stood at the cliff. There was no one around. Maybe I was doing this to give myself a mood boost. Or maybe I was envious of the environment, the greenery around. Nature is always beautiful, even in the coldest period. I longed for that too, and I never knew what I could do, at least to make me as close as possible to Mother Nature. The icy winds seized hold of me, blowing out my woollen shawl as though trying to force me to return, to go back to my house.

But I had decided.

I wanted a change in my life. I wanted to change my life, and I wanted it fast. If happiness cannot come to me, then I am going to find it in another world. I was standing at the tip of the mountain. There was darkness and a dense forest below.

I closed my eyes, stretched my arms sideways.

Now, what's this? What's happening? My entire body began to vibrate. I searched my trouser's side pockets. What's this? Mobile! I cursed myself. Now, who brings mobile in the final moments? Yet, curiosity prompted me to have a last look at the mobile screen.
Who could it be?

***

Suraj Singh. My college boyfriend from Delhi. He was the most exciting person I knew. I was always laughing when with him. He had such lovely brows that I couldn't stop staring at him. His skin was always moist as if he had just come out of the gym. We were a couple to be admired. Each time we were together, he would sing to me. Suraj had a philosophy and lived by it. "We are alive because we should live," he would often say.

I was happiest when we were together. But like any other good thing in life, even our relationship had an expiry date.

What could he possibly want with me after twenty years? His text was strange and something I wasn't expecting – not from him, not from anyone. It appeared to be a day of strange occurrences. Should I reply to him? But what's the point? I am sure I wouldn't be around before he responds. Suraj had shared a photo of us from my twenty-first birthday. We had gone to Agra to make the Taj Mahal, an ivory-white marble mausoleum, a symbol of pure love as a witness to our love.

I loved Suraj for being so thoughtful and sweet. The Taj Mahal and I were celebrating our precious love on that day. It felt magical being twenty-one. Seeing that photo reminded me of the sweet moments. I never loved anyone the way I did, Suraj. He was adorable in every aspect, and I always fantasized about growing old with him.

"Helloow, Sunshine! If this reaches you, you know what to do." That was the caption on the shared image.

He loved doing that to me back when we were dating. Once, on the pretext of going on a college trip, I went with him, and we lived together for 15 days in a cottage near Sariska, the wildlife sanctuary. He would wake up before me and make breakfast; he would then leave these notes from the bed to the bathroom, saying something sweet about me, anything that would boost my moods. And right he was. These small gestures made me feel loved and alive.

On the other hand, I was the best he ever saw. We were together since our school days. Suraj would sometimes call me when he was alone in his hostel room, telling me how he had missed me. What he had with me was found nowhere else. We were perfect for each other. At least for the time it lasted. But over two decades had passed since we last saw each other. Ever since he finished his post-graduation in Commerce from Delhi University and me – B.Ed, teacher's training course, Suraj and I grew distant. His father, Patel Singh, was the owner of Singh Hotels & Motels, the famous chain of 5-star hotels in Delhi and Mumbai. Suraj was made the heir. He had to share the responsibility. "No more studies." He was ordered.

Being made sole heir to the large empire was not the problem. His father put a condition that was just like revisiting the Mahabharata and meeting characters coming alive from the epic who always laid a condition that made the other helpless and feeble. His father told him that he had to marry Neha Jadeja, the daughter of his rival business partner. Marriage was supposed to erase the traces of rivalry if any. It was a business alliance.

Suraj had no option.

Suraj had dreamt of inheriting the empire from his father one day. He went to school for that sole purpose, gaining knowledge to run the business empire when he came of age. That was his purpose in life, and Suraj was always excited when he went to work at Singh Hotels during the holidays. He wanted to make a difference, infuse new blood in the old competitive dwindling empire.

It was on a Friday night when Suraj approached me and asked if we could have a moment. At first, I thought he would propose to me because he was never that serious about things. A rich spoilt brat – you may call him. But I loved him. Our relationship was booming, and I was waiting for him to propose and say yes.

"I have news but am not sure if it would be bad or good news - only you can tell," he said with profound quietude.

"Propose already!" I interrupted with a refreshing smile. Suraj didn't react. His face wore an expressionless look. I felt something turn in my stomach. My body was suddenly cold, and I felt life escape me. Something was wrong, and judging by how am feeling, it wasn't something good. Does he want to leave me? What did I do? We were in love, right?

"It is about something I have been pondering about for a while, but...." Suraj paused for a moment and wiped a tear that was rolling down his cheek. I could feel how heavy whatever he wanted to tell me weighed on his shoulders. The room had become a graveyard, silent. It was so quiet that I could hear Suraj's breathing. It was heavy and deep.

"You know how much I had wanted to inherit my father's company," he said, "today, my father called me to let me know that it was time for me to inherit the company."

At that time, I wondered how that could be bad news for anyone. At best, I would be his woman. At worst- there is no worst. I thought of only good things coming out of such news. Life would be simpler and expensive from there.

"My father told me that I'm to inherit the company if I agree to marry Neha, uncle Jadeja's daughter." Said Suraj as he reached for my arm.

I pulled away and succumbed to shock. I couldn't believe he chose his company over me. Judging from how he was telling me about what transpired, it was clear he meant to inform me but never to have a discussion. How could he? People who love each other always talk about these things, but he decided to end everything without discussing it. My breath stopped, and eyes miserably failed to control emotions. I could feel tears rolling down my cheeks to the neck. With face experiencing a wet weekend, I could barely stand. I gave a loud outcry. I was crushed to the bone, and I hated Suraj for it. He tried comforting me, but there was nothing he would do or say that could have made me feel better.

As I got engulfed by the nostalgic wave of romance, older romance, I wondered if I should reply to him. My time had come to an end, and his resurfacing was pointless - at least to me. I thought of not replying because it would start a fire that cannot be put out. He will get the news of my death and know why I didn't reply to him. It was better that way. My time with Suraj was bitter-sweet, and as much as it crossed my mind that it may be the start of something new, I knew I was overreaching, and it wasn't worth the effort. I put the phone back in my pocket. I wanted to have one last look at the mountains. Perhaps as a ghost, I would return to this town and get lost in the eccentric view. It was satisfying looking at nature's beauty. The sun had heated the dewdrops on the surfaces. Above, hair-like clouds painted the blue sky with a shed of white, making it look like a canvas by Picasso. The sun's rays warmed my skin, and I felt the cold slip away; like thawing ice, I got warmer.

I loved how I was feeling, and I wanted to take that memory with me. I began thinking about Surr – yes, that's what I used to call him. But why am I calling by this name today? Why today? And why was he texting me on this particular day? It had been a long time, and how does he even think I still have feelings for him? Surr's texts were always like that. He would say something optimistic and vague. How was I to know what I was to do? Does he expect me to call him? Or a simple reply would suffice—a simple "hello" text. Part of me was glad that even after these years, Surr still thinks of me. The way he had texted me was something I had never seen pop up on my screen for years.

'What if he needs you?' A tiny little voice pricked me. *'You're his ex-flame!'* After all, *ex-ses* seem to have that control, much after they have disappeared from your private space! My fingers clicked on the WhatsApp message. I postponed my decision.

I returned without fulfilling my mission. Rishabh, my husband, had already gone to his shop. The house was empty, and I needed to be alone.

I decided to write something that pictures what was in my mind. I wanted people to know what I felt, how I have been feeling, what compelled me into doing what I planned. I wanted them to know everything to help someone out there who is in the same ocean as me. I wouldn't wish what I went through to anyone.

But death could wait for now.

I decided to sort out Suraj's issue first.

***

I sat down at the table in the corner of a small hotel on the city's outskirts. Suraj was nowhere, but the table was laid ready for lunch. I took off my scarf.

“You look still the same.”

The same voice. I turned my neck violently. “You? Where were you? I didn’t see you enter.”

He sat opposite me and gave me a broad grin. “I was behind the reception counter. This is my hotel.”

“Oh! No wonder!” There was a bit of anger in my voice. “So, Mr Owner of this hotel, would you please tell me why did you want to meet me and how the hell did you know that I was living here in Almora?”

“Can we eat something? Will answer your questions and you have every right to speak to me like that.”

“No, I’ve no right on you and don’t give me this shit after twenty years,” I replied.

He suddenly lost sight of all external things, caught my hand, dragged me up from the chair and ordered his staff to get him food in his hotel room. I never expected this.

Once inside the room, he pushed me into the chair, sat on the floor and kept his head on my lap. I couldn't refuse. I patiently listened to his story. I couldn't see his face. Only felt the dampness around my knees, tears trickling even below the thick material of my old jeans.

He got up, looked into my eyes. I turned away, but it was useless for me to avoid him; the image of a woman, his so-called wife he had painted, just now reflected in my mind as in his eyes. I tried to break it into a thousand fragments, but each fragment of his story retained that image of his solitude and pain. Something hit me. It reminded me of my marital status.

I picked up my handbag. "Please do not expect me again. It is better for us to free ourselves of each other's existence and not sink to the bottom to hurt so many other people. I'm coming to you no more. Forget me, do not message me, and do not see me again."

"Rakhee, I've missed you all this while. You can't punish me and continue to suffer. You just cannot think about dying."

I froze.

"Sorry. The local constable who got your husband back home the other day told me. And in the morning, I saw you at the cliff, and if I'm not wrong, you were attempting suicide."

I didn't look back. I returned without saying anything. I was determined never to see him again.

***

While basking in the glory of the sunset, I saw my husband approaching from a distance. I began wondering why he is back so soon. He always said he is going for an hour but never returned till late at night and that too somebody had to bring him back. Does he know that I went to meet Suraj?

I could see that he had trimmed his hair and shaved his beard. Rishabh had worn the same coat that I had presented him many years ago. He looked handsome. I could feel joy in my heart trying to surface. I then noticed him smiling at me. His teeth were not as white, but the awe of his smile remained.

What was happening? I had no idea.

I quickly snapped myself out of the limbo I was in to focus on the current events. I wondered why Rishabh groomed up suddenly. Then I realized how tamed he had been. From the moment I shouted back at him and refused to make him dinner last evening, my husband was never the same again. I was too angry to acknowledge it, but I struck a nerve.

"I want to apologize for how I have treated you lately, "said Rishabh. He was now standing beside where I was. I was shocked by what he said, and I noticed that his hands were behind him. I knew he had flowers in his hands – possibly my favourite; yellow roses. I did not know what was wrong with everyone. I just wanted to die in peace.

"Please, leave me alone." I was rude. "Just go inside and do whatever you want to do. And... and leave the flowers!" I said as I turned my face away and closed my eyes, and continued to feel the warmth of the sunset.

Rishabh stood there, glued for a moment, and said three words. "I love you."

He left the flowers with me and went inside the house.

On the day I had decided to leave this world, all the men in my life thought it best to notice that I existed!

Ping!

That was my Facebook notification tone. Who is bothering me at such a moment? I always hated it when I hear a notification alert and get excited to see something interesting – only to find that it's a notification about someone liking a photo I liked a while back. I always feel drained in such instances. It might as well be one of such instances. I decided not to check whatever was lying on the other side of the notification.

Then, my Facebook notification alert tone rang for the second time. This time, it got my attention and perking interest. I wasn't that popular getting two notifications in a row – not saying the same day. I left teaching many years ago. In any case, I was not very popular with my students. So, who could it be? Something must be up.

Suraj?

I went for my phone that was on the chair behind me.

***

His lips had always been soft, but not this softness. It was as if they were smeared with olive oil – slippery. As he sucked my lower lip, his hands grabbed me tightly. My heart was racing at this point, the tension, the closeness - I had never felt like that in ages. “Surr…!” I whispered. I felt a chill down my spine accompanied by an overwhelming feeling from within my chest - it was incendiary. I felt alive.

“All these years, I missed you terribly, Rakhee.” He pulled me closer, and I wrapped my hands around his shoulders. I wanted to feel his warmth. I wanted to feel him. “For twenty years, I kept cursing the day I let you go and accepted Dad’s blind offer.”

"I had missed you, too," I said as I grabbed him by the neck, looking at his eyes. The view was satisfying. He had a longing in him, a desire. I found myself taking a deep, slow breath. My emotions were all over the place. I didn't want him to stop. I was in the seventh heaven. I think I could feel the blood flowing in my veins. My whole body was sensitive.

"I love you," he said while removing his hand from my waist and held me by my face. His hand felt warm and soft. I didn't want to open my eyes. I just wanted to experience every bit.

“I love you, too.” I softly whispered in his ear.

This had been the routine for Surr and me. I loved every moment we spent at Ecstasy Lodge. Room 321 was reserved for us each Thursday. Since it was out of town, we would travel separately as we both had keys to the room. As married people, we knew it was wrong, but it felt right for us. I, for one, had gone through a lot and I deserved feeling good for once. At this point, I wasn't focusing on right or wrong; moral or not – ardour defined my actions. And I adored being with him in that room. I endeared what we did. The scheduled Thursdays seemed years apart. After we parted, my consciousness was left in that room. All I could think about for the rest of the days until I see him again was to meet him, to be with him.

"What about your husband?" said Surr as he wore his black leather belt. It had a big silver buckle with the initials *'Louis Vuitton'* engraved. It had an expensive look.

Does he know about us? My inner voice alerted me.

"What about him?" I asked while putting him off. I never wanted to talk about my husband or my suicidal attempts. This was the second time my efforts went to drain, and I had started to feel like the universe did not want me dead. Earlier, Surr and I had talked about why I wanted to meet my God.

"I never thought you're such a coward." He had said and kept on lamenting that I had no right to do that; only God gives and takes life. I understood where he came from, understood his argument. There was only one flaw; he hadn't been what I went through. I had not yet told him how I had two miscarriages, one stillborn, and a six-month dead son. Maybe he cannot understand it all, but I was in hell.

No one can understand where I was, even if they try. I sometimes questioned if I was supposed to come to this world. I couldn't be the one to take everything terrible the world has to offer. I also deserve some good time like everybody else.

Surr ignored my question because he knew it was useless to argue with me on this issue and stretched out his arm towards me.

"Shall we go?" He asked.

Surr had always been a gentleman – that sweet friend, that romantic lover, perfect husband, I longed for. He had a smile that was bright and energetic. I could feel a change of mood whenever we had a conversation. I adored his infectious positive energy. Then, I tilted my head towards my shoulder while pulling my shoulder towards my tilting head; my facial expression disapproved of his offer. I wanted to see what he would do. Surr smiled and nodded his head, and in quick succession, he took a step forward and grabbed me by my waist and back – carrying me like a plank of wood. It felt good, and I couldn't stop laughing. Surr swung me around before putting me down. We were so close that I could hear him breathing. His arms were around me, and my hands pressed against his chest. With his height, my head would perfectly rest on his shoulder.

"You still weigh the same." He said putting me down on the floor.

I smiled.

"Let's go," whispered Surr. I didn't want to leave his side. I am sure Surr also felt the same way. Even after telling us to leave, his grip was still tight; I couldn't go even if I wanted to. So, we stayed there for about five minutes – nobody saying anything to the other. We dragged the moment for as long as we could because it was magical.

***

Back at home, my husband was in the sitting room watching an old romantic movie – *Kuch Kuch Hota Hai* on an OTT platform. As newlyweds, we used to watch that movie every Sunday of the first month. It was a ritual, and each time, we would try to see if there was something we missed during our previous watch. It was fun and diverting. Seeing him on the couch, I wondered why he even decided to watch it.

My husband had changed to a different man. He was home before the sunset, and during the weekends, he would sleep next to the cedar hedge trees at the back of our house. At least thrice, he had confronted me about resolving issues with him. He said that he saw the error of his ways and was ready to start afresh. Indeed, Rishabh was a different person. He was sober every day. He had stopped alcohol completely. It was a mystery. His routine for getting drunk had been destructive. I thought he needed rehabilitation or anything that would pull him away from the jaws of alcohol addiction. But he stopped taking alcohol the way he had begun drinking – suddenly. And he seemed fine. If you didn't know, you wouldn't believe if it was the same man in muddy clothes a few weeks back; the village drunk. Even his skin had begun to gleam and his eyes whitening.

In my mind, I rejected the idea of us being together, but I couldn't leave him either. He had me through the nether regions, and I couldn't just pretend all that did not happen. We all went through agonizing times when Anand passed away. After my first miscarriage, I had Anand, and Rishabh gave him that name because Anand was our key to happiness. He brought laughter to our lives. Having been married for four years, it was a perfect time, and my son made me forget about the lost one. There would have been two children in our house if there had been no miscarriage.

Nonetheless, I felt a brightness in me that gave me the strength to move on with life. But my happiness was short-lived. Anand died at six months. I felt reaped apart, and all that pain that was distracted by Anand came flooding. I wouldn't eat or do anything for a few months. My health deteriorated, and I lost more than twenty kilograms.

Rishabh was with me through it all. He helped cook for me; wash my body – he was my caregiver. During this time, he used to drink a few glasses each night. I didn't notice it initially, but when I did, I understood it must be hard for him to bear the pain of losing a child alone and have to nurse his wife. These few glasses progressed to a bottle, and it was slippery onwards. Rishabh lost control of himself the day he knew I was in a good mental state. I was okay with it at first since I already had my episode. And like a good wife, I used what I had to make him come closer to me.

Physical intimacy was the strategy I chose initially, and I now regret it. Up to that point, we only had one miscarriage and one dead son. As much as that pain disrupted my sanity, I only had scratched the surface. We used to make love thrice a week, and my husband was slowly coming back to me. Then out of nowhere, I got pregnant again. Rishabh was thrilled and gave the child a name even before he was born. Akshara was the name, and he would ask about the baby's health each day.

"How do you know it's going to be a girl?" I would often pester him.

"I just know." This was his simple answer.

Over a period of time, it became clear to me that Rishabh was more worried about the baby than me. It felt heavenly, though, seeing him respond to all my demands. Even if in the middle of the night I would say *Akshara is in the mood for thandai,* he would go and get me some. It was fulfilling, and I loved the pampering. But then came the stillborn, followed by another miscarriage. Rishabh must have lost in when we had our last miscarriage. He was drinking himself to death. This was when I would go fetch him – from the trench – he found himself that night or would go running out as soon as the local police officers rang up and complained, "Ma'am come soon, or we will have to put him behind bars."

I understood his torture while dealing with my own. As days and weeks went by, years accumulated, and Rishabh never seemed to back down anytime soon. Feeling lonely and abandoned, I began hating him for what he was doing. The torment I had inside me was enough. He shouldn't add any more.

"How was your day?" asked Rishabh. "I brought you chicken. I think we should make chicken curry for dinner."

Rishabh knew I loved chicken curry. When you add the spices just a little bit more than the usual quantities, the explosion in the mouth is heavenly. I just smiled and looked at him. He knew how to focus my attention on him. The movie and now the request. I knew he was up to something. I nodded, signifying I agreed to the plan, and went to the bedroom to freshen up before cooking.

While in the shower, I heard Rishabh enter our

master bedroom. I was afraid that he would come inside and want us to share a bath. I knew he wanted me, but I did not. I hadn't been comfortable with him to that extent. I needed time. He had been to hell and back. I still hadn't known what made him come back to his senses. I perceived that I was the reason. But I didn't want to address the issue. I had a good thing going on with Surr; I loved them both equally and differently.

Rishabh's footsteps stopped at the bathroom door, and I felt the door squeak a little. My heart was pounding, and I wasn't sure how to react. Water was flowing from the shower, and my reflexes forced my hand on the shower tap. Then it struck me if I did that, then he would know that I have acknowledged his presence, and I would be forced to speak anything or be ready for what would follow next. I froze my hand quickly and remained still. Rishabh also stood at the door as if in a dilemma himself. Should he come inside or go away. Ten seconds later, the anxiety and tension were too much for me.

Rishabh moved away from the bathroom door and went to the sitting room. He made sure he moved in stealth. I stayed in the bathroom for some more time but he never came back. I dressed up and went to the kitchen.

"That's a new record even for you," said Rishabh while he smiled at me. "You took forty-five minutes just taking a shower today. New record."

Dubiety drowned me as I did not know if Rishabh was at the bathroom door or I had imagined it. How he spoke did not show any signs that he was in the room with me. I wanted to ask him about it but stopped myself. What if I was losing my mind? What if it was true and brought out an awkwardness that would spoil the mood? I then told myself I should just let it go and adapt to the mood. I looked at him and smiled once again. If he were outside the bathroom, he would understand we are not there yet. I went ahead to prepare the chicken curry.

"I want you to know that I am here now. I am here for you and never would leave your side," said Rishabh, who was now at the kitchen door. Looking at his eyes, I knew he meant that. His voice was shaky and deep. He always had that when he was nervous about anything but still had to talk.

Rishabh, my husband, had come back to me after all these years. I was delighted by that and kept on wishing the timing wasn't this bad. Inside, I had a hurricane of emotions. My heart melted upon seeing the necklace in his hand. It was beautiful. It had tiny diamonds on its hexagonal pendant that housed a heart. With its glittering ambience, I couldn't stop staring at it and imagining how it would hang on my neck. I was speechless, and tears started to roll down my cheeks. Seeing that,

Rishabh advanced to where I was and hugged me. His muscles were still attached to his chest. Though not as stiff as they used to be, the protrusion felt like little sponges. I was comfortable and forgot that I didn't want him close to me minutes ago.

"I love you," he said while kissing me on the forehead. I was still speechless until he wore the necklace around my neck. At this point, I couldn't feel myself, and deep down, I knew I was vulnerable. Rishabh knew what to do to get what he wanted with me. I was his slave when he wanted, and I loved that. Being close to him felt strange but necessary. I wanted to stay because he was so sweet, and I felt like I could do anything for him. At the same time, I wasn't over what he put me through. For that reason, I also wanted to leave his side. In a dilemma of my own, I was glued there. Then I saw his hands reaching for my face. Rishabh wanted to kiss me. His timing was perfect as I wasn't able to resist that. I didn't want it to happen but couldn't stop it from happening. I began regretting why I get carried away that fast.

"*Pangg*!!"

The lid covering the *Kadhai* (pot) with chicken curry fell off. The pressure from boiling soup beneath was too great. I felt a relief because I knew I would now divert my attention and prevent myself from something I did not want to happen. I left my husband's presence and rushed to the gas stove.

I was lucky.

My husband, Rishabh, stood there for a short while before leaving the kitchen. I pretended to be busy ensuring the meal came out delicious, but we both knew I avoided him. That was his chance to attempt anything, and it was lost. He would have to develop something else that would trick me, like how he managed moments ago. I looked at the necklace on my neck.

***

Eight months had passed, and I was now in a love triangle – my husband and Surr included. I would disappear every Thursday to be with Surr in his beautiful nest. I would give numerous excuses about my whereabouts at home, and I always suspected that Rishabh knew I was lying. But, I still did it because I couldn't imagine going for more than a week without seeing Surr. I had feelings for him, and the thrill of us having a gateway to drive ourselves crazy was irresistible. I also loved Rishabh, my husband, dearly because I couldn't imagine life without him. He was not perfect, but I loved how he came out of his prison unscathed. He was mentally tough, and if he determined to get something, he would go all out to get it. That was what made me be with him despite what happened. We had reconciled but were not as free with each other as I was with

Surr. Part of me was still teaching him a lesson, and another part wanted him to know that I still cared for him. We still had our sanity despite what happened. I was scared that if I get intimate with him, I will lose Suraj or both. I didn't want that. So, I let things flow like a river, bending at will while adjusting to the oncoming waves.

Surr, on the other hand, was obsessed with me. He would text me on Facebook almost every 10 minutes. I loved the attention, and he made me feel like the centre of his life. He would sometimes send a message while I was with Rishabh, and I would have to find a reason to go to the kitchen or to the washroom to check what Surr had sent.

Life had taken a strange turn that I never thought would be possible. A few months ago, I thought about leaving this world for the next – but I am alive and happy. I had been given a second chance at happiness and wanted to enjoy it as much as possible – while it lasted. On that day, Surr had texted me while I was with Rishabh watching our favourite movie, *Kuch Kuch Hota Hai*. I had sat in front of Rishabh, who had opened his legs to accommodate me in between. My back leaned on him, and I was the one with the remote control. My phone was at the table – a stone's throw away. There was a beep, and I knew it would be Surr, as I had customized the beep sound. I pretended not to have heard the message alert and continued watching the movie. About ten minutes later, I stood and reached for my phone before heading to the washroom.

I was eager to see what Surr had sent me. In my mind, I couldn't stop imagining how his facial expression would be like when saying what he wrote in the message. Whenever I talked to him over the phone, I would fantasize about how an actual conversation would be. I was in love with the idea, and it made me happy. *Tomorrow 10 am* – read the text. A smile wore my face, and I began fantasizing about his touch. I loved it when he caressed me. After a while, I flushed the toilet even though I had done nothing related and left. While heading back to the sitting room, I went to the window and saw the moon shining brightly.

It was a Wednesday night, and the sky was rich in blue. The gentle breeze outside gave a refreshing mood and blew the linen curtains. The dry leaves on the ground also made small leaps as the zephyr dominated. I looked back. Rishabh had put the movie on pause and was in the kitchen. The breeze made the rope that I had made Rishabh hung some months ago also swung. It made me remember the conversation that we both had that day.

***

"There is a rope in the kitchen. Can you tie it to that pole over there?" I had asked Rishabh and pointed to the pole at the centre of our house, "I want to do something?"

"What business do you have with ropes?" Rishabh had asked with a frown on his face and anxiety in his voice.

"Did I ever ask you where you were going? Let's just stay out of each other's hair. I think that way it will be good for us. Just fix the rope for me."

"Yes, the rope!" he said and looked for a stool.

The stool was beside the ironing board, with a heap of clothes on top, waiting to be folded. Rishabh placed the clothes on the couch and fixed the rope. He then did something that I had never seen him do – returning the stool to where he found it and meticulously put the clothes back on it.

***

I didn't believe it was still there, let alone imagining that I was the same person thinking of ending my life. Did Rishabh guess my motive that day? Did that incident change him? I don't know and wouldn't like to know, either.

My life had moved a full circle. It was now sweet and sour. Beautiful and content. I looked at my phone and smiled. I had an appointment, and in front of me was Rishabh, waiting for me to join him. I guess, sometimes in life, once is not enough. It gives us opportunities to make choices. Nothing ends until it ends. Like now!

■

The Singer

Families can be challenging.

We might disagree on things and often find ourselves on each others' throats. This phenomenon is distasteful, and I wouldn't say I like it when a family is divided. To me, no reason can justify a family being at war with each other. The world already is an unfair playing field that requires solid familial bonds to help a person cruise through life. At least I need that, but not for everyone. Others prefer the feuds that result in an endless conflict between family members. This happens, and this world has come to normalise family feuds. I haven't reached that point yet and never wish to. I don't like it when a family is drawn apart because of something that can be resolved through an intervention. But, we cannot ignore that most people nowadays have lasting feuds with their family members. I know a few, and I am sure you also know a few if you already are not part of feuding family members. It is a story of this family that I know. Their feud is not like anything I had seen before. This family often finds something to argue. Each member of the family has a face beneath the visible face. The Kumar family comprises four people – Bhavna, Ajit and their two children, Atul and Seema. They argue, fight. The reason? I don't know. You read and do let me know.

"Where's the remote?" I said while looking around

the table and couches, "and can someone fetch me my ash tray from the bedroom." Then, I looked at my teenage daughter while signalling her with a hand gesture that reinforced what I had just said. "Are you deaf or something?" I added while going after her.

Seema thought she owned the television and she would hide the remote after putting on her favourite channel. I was not in the mood today. I wanted to look at my favourite show, *Faces* – a repeat telecast. About twenty years ago, people were as eager watching me grab the mic and drive them crazy with my voice. I was the best, and everybody knew it. And this happened because of the serial *Faces* that the world got to know me.

Back then, in the 1990s, singing was a talent that needed to choose you. Not everyone could sing like today. There were only a few talented people that could bring out emotions through their voices. My *gurus* at the university praised me. They blessed me. They promoted me.

Today, most people love the auto-tuning musicians and call that a beautiful voice. That's just rubbish and nothing to be proud of. Then you would hear they have millions of likes on social media. Why?

"I think I asked you where the remote is? I don't want to repeat myself. Give it to me!" I shouted at

Seema. "Atul, bring me the ash tray," I added with more volume. I wondered why I was given these two as children. Teenagers are just a load of problems.

"Damn it, Seema, is this the modernity you've been yapping about since you've begun to grow like a palm tree? Give me the remote."

While Bhavna was yelling at her daughter, Seema was lost in thoughts. She had always been jealous of her mother. Her mother, Bhavna, had beautiful eyes and long dark hair. Even in her fifties, men looked at her when they went shopping. Seema hated it.

"Fine," replied Seema and threw the remote at me.

As I picked up the remote from the floor, I wondered what I wasn't doing as a mother to make these children happy. Seema was always angry and always dodged me when I want to bond with her. The last time I asked her we go shopping, she never wore the clothes we bought on that day. Atul is always in his room. No one knows what he's doing inside there because his door is always locked. I tried telling him not to lock his door because he shouldn't have anything to hide, but his father allowed him to do what he wanted.

I sat down, but all the enthusiasm to watch *Faces* had melted away. I was no longer interested in listening to my voice. My mind wandered to a distant past when I had just returned from Delhi. My mother was sick at that time, and she was bedridden. I was her caregiver for two weeks before she passed away. Her death changed my life in many ways. Her dying wish was that I should follow my dream. While at her death bed, I used to sing her favourite filmy songs. She believed I was talented and wished I pursue my dream. But she put a condition that I should get married first.

"You're going to be 30 soon. Get married. I'm going. Your father already has so many problems on his head. Get married." She had said.

Hearing her speak those words was too emotional for me, and I couldn't stay beside her. I wanted her to stay with me until I achieved success. I needed her by my side to fulfill my dream. But she was in a hurry to go. And I don't blame her. She was suffering. After all, how much pain can one endure!

I didn't want her to notice my moist eyes. I rushed to the bathroom to cry my heart out. When I came back five minutes later, my mother was gone, and I never got the chance to say goodbye. I was devastated from the inside out and couldn't think I would get through that phase. But I wanted to honour her last wish. I began to knock at the doors of the music directors, sought help from my gurus and with their recommendations, soon the destiny smiled at me. Things opened up for me, starting with the serial – *Faces.* It set my path to stardom. Everybody said, "Goddess Saraswati has blessed you."

Before you think it has been a ride to the sunset, life has been the worst for me since I got married. I wish I had known his darkest secret before saying yes eagerly. I wouldn't be here right now. If I were to describe the words that portray my marriage, a black hole would tell my twenty years of marriage. All it has done is take and have nothing to offer back. The only good thing marriage gave me was my two children. I loved them with all my heart. I wasn't sure they felt the same way about me, but I was grateful for them deep down. In the house, they were my source of happiness. Seeing their faces each day gave me the strength to be in that house. They made me want to push through the thick canopies of life. Not my husband. We were apart than we were together. Even a mundane conversation about a non-existent issue would prompt us to slit each other's throats. See, all this time I was arguing with Seema, he was seated on the other side of the room, quiet as if nothing was happening and even when he talked there apathy in his voice. He was there, yet not with me.

Ajit Kumar, the sound studio owner, and I married soon after my mother passed away. I thought we would build our life together. Everybody envied us – "What a couple! Studio owner and a singer."
I believed their words!

Ajit was from Singapore. He did a course in

audio engineering. His wealthy parents helped him set up his audio studio. And I was young and ambitious. My mother had just passed away, and when the opportunity to marry him came, I grabbed it. Looking back, I wish I had not. Ajit did not have eyes for me. We pretended to be a happy couple before people all these years, but we were odd ducks in reality. Ajit even proposed artificial insemination when I told him I wanted kids. "Medical science has advanced. Go ahead and do it," he said and willingly accompanied me to the clinic.

While Bhavna was seated contemplating her miserable life, her daughter came from her room to see what her mother was watching. Not because she wanted to watch the program, but just to see if her mother was watching what she said. Upon seeing the same programme she had selected earlier, she looked at her mother with disbelief. Seema then went to sit beside her mother and took the remote from her. Bhavna was not even concentrating on Seema's actions. She had been captivated in her river of sadness and loneliness. Bhavna longed for someone to see her for who she was; a loving and energetic woman. For most of her marriage, her husband has had nothing to do with her. Bhavna went to rehab at least four times, but she was still back at smoking and drinking. She said it helped keep her sane because she would round the bend when left without her favourite toys. In the living room, Bhavna held a cigarette between her fingers. As much as Seema hated her mother for having all the good

genes, she empathized with her. She felt her pain. At that moment, she knew her mother was having one of her episodes and leaned towards her, laying her head on her lap and stayed there. Seeing that, Bhavna was brought back from her universe.

"Can you please bring me my ash tray? I feel like I'm running mad with your brother." I said while whispering to my daughter. Sometimes she would be nice, and we would have unforgettable times. When she turned fifteen, we both baked the cake, and I could tell she was happy. Unfortunately, it was the same day we went shopping, and that was where our good day was ruined.

"I was waiting to see when Atul would bring you your ash tray. He doesn't even hear you while in his room," said Seema. I then looked back and saw my husband, who was now at the kitchen counter on his phone. If Ajit was not in his studio, he was on his phone – probably talking with his lover. It stung deep inside, and I wished life had chosen a different path for me. I was raised by a family that appreciated familial bond and honour. My father always told me that everything would be fine. I did what he said, but things were far from being satisfactory.

"Here." She gave me the ash tray and added, "You look miserable when thinking. You'll fall sick."

Seema's words were uplifting for me. Though in her complex ways, she expressed her care for my health. I always thought Seema knew my troubles but pretended not to. I never asked her because I cannot start explaining everything to her. She was still young, and I wanted her to reach eighteen before explaining everything to her. Atul was a problematic child. I couldn't reach him. He loved locking himself up in his room. When it wasn't a school day, he wouldn't come out until it was time to eat. Even then, Atul would sometimes ask for the house helper to bring him food. I didn't like it, but his father condoned the behaviour. What he did in his room all alone – I don't know but yes, sometimes I experienced peculiar smell emanating from his room.

Then, Atul's footsteps could be heard. Both Bhavna and Seema looked in the direction he was coming from. Bhavna took a lighter from her pyjama pockets and lit her cigarette.

"What was it mum, the whole neighbourhood now knows you smoke. Isn't that your tray with you, in your hands? Why is everyone against me in this house?" He threw a condescending glance at me and continued to rant about why everyone in the house did not understand him.

"Get a girlfriend if you want someone to love you. Don't disturb our peace. And mum, didn't they teach you never to smoke around your children?" Seema, who was now sitting up to start a confrontation with her brother, attacked me. They loved fighting all the time, and I hated it.

"Watch it, Seema!" I said while giving Seema a stern look. "And you, if you heard me, why were you still in your room. Understand others if you want to be understood."

Then I got up and headed outside on the balcony to continue smoking. With tray in one hand and cigarette in the other, I smoked my sorrows away. I had envisioned a different life for myself, my marriage, and my family.

The day I went shopping with my daughter made me realize I was a lonely mother. Then, I remembered meeting an old friend, Vivaan. He and I had dated during our college days. Seeing him as handsome as ever, I thought of how he used to hold and touch me. It had been more than twenty years, but I still remembered.

Two decades down the line, I stopped singing. There was no one to share my life. Sometimes I wish I would take anyone from the road when I have my episodes, but I think again, and the faces of my children, sniggering colleagues, my mother's face and my upbringing pass through my eyes. Our relationship and familial bond were on the rocks. I did not want to add salt to that. As the smoke filled my lungs, I could feel my head becoming lighter. Blood started flowing in my veins, and all my thoughts began falling off like bats off a branch.

My problems began to feel less heavy on my shoulders. Life cruised through my veins, and I felt better once more. I knew my happiness would last as long as the lighted cigarette was in between my fingers. Though, a brief moment, I always wished it to last forever!

Ping...

I took out the phone from my pocket and looked at the notifications.

Vivaan's text was the first, and he was complaining about his mental health. He had been diagnosed with depression and insomnia. "Oh, no!" Inadvertently the words tumbled out.

"What happened?" Seema asked from the living room.

"Nothing." I recollected and replied.

I hadn't gone to a psychiatrist, but I was sure to have multiple conditions from substance dependence to depression. But with every puff, I knew it was going to be a bumpy ride. While on the balcony of our penthouse in Mumbai, I looked at the city ahead and wondered if I was the only one suffering. My life needed that spark to keep me going. I thought of helping Vivaan while giving myself something to keep me distracted, at least for now.

The future is always uncertain, and we all know that.
I craved and desperately wanted love and affection.

I hadn't had much fun with my sexual life. His eyes only saw men. He found comfort at the hands of other men, and when we married, he told me about his secret. He wanted me to know but still keep it a secret. Ajit had told me to find someone who would satisfy my sexual needs. I thought I would change him. Maybe he needed a change of perspective, and I dedicated 20 precious years of my life trying to transform him. But I failed. I only succeeded in changing my life. Music flew away from my life.

Bhavna was growing old, and she longed for someone to give her attention for once. For twenty years, she had been faithful to a marriage that had no meaning. A marriage that was held together by ambition. No romance, only aspirations to leave a legacy behind. In addition to honouring her mother's wish, Bhavna agreed to marry Ajit because she knew that her music career would burgeon with him as her partner. And it did, but she was not happy. She bargained love and happiness to become a singing sensation. And by the time she realised that life was not all about the money and the fame, it was too late. She blamed herself for Ma Saraswati abandoning her; musical notes going haywire and music directors avoiding her. She was unhappy and it reflected in her work.
Bhavna regretted a lot of choices she made during her

youthful years. She missed a lot of things. A kiss, for instance. She had forgotten how it feels to be a woman; to be desired. It had been such a long time!

▬

The Birthday Cake

Akash sat in the corner of his room. Tears blurring his vision. His parents had not come home again. They had promised to be there for his birthday but had not come. It was not like he was not proud of his parents. But surely they could have come for his birthday at least.

The COVID-19 pandemic had taken over the whole world in its grasp. Thousands of people had died, and hundreds of thousands were sick due to the virus. They were put in quarantine for 15 days to avoid further spread. Even then, the pandemic had not stopped. His parents, both doctors, had not been able to come home for more than a week now. He missed them a lot, but he could not complain. They had not come to keep them safe. As they were always around COVID patients, they were at a high risk of getting infected. If they were infected, there was a chance of him and his twin sisters, Irshita and Ishani, getting infected.

His sisters and Renu Kaki, the housekeeper, had prepared a cake for his birthday. But he had not come out of room to celebrate it. He wanted his parents to be home. He got up to go to bed when he heard a knock on the door, "Akash, it's mom and dad," Irshita said while winking at Ishani. They both wanted their little brother to open the door.

"Go away. I don't want to talk to anyone." It was not true, though. He wanted someone to come to him. His sisters or his parents. Even if he was angry, he wanted someone to talk to. He was alone, and he felt lonely every second. When everything had been normal, they used to talk to each other every day. Every weekend they would go to a picnic and enjoy. They were happy, then.

He felt like crying, but he did not want to. He tried to be strong, as he knew that his parents were doing their duty. They were working day and night to save lives. They were his superheroes. No superhero came to help the world when people were falling sick of COVID-19. Only his parents and other doctors like them took the duty of saving lives. They were real-life superheroes. Even though their own life was at stake, they did not back out. They stayed and helped people fight the disease. He was a proud son.

But even then, he was just a kid – 10-year old. He needed his parents to console him. He needed them by his side. He needed to see their faces every day. He needed to hear their voices, and talking to them on call was not enough.

Irshita knocked on the door again, and this time he could hear Ishani, her twin, as well. He went to the door and opened it to let them in. They walked in and went to sit on his bed. He sat on his bed, between the two.

"Don't be so grumpy. We are on your side," Ishani said consoling him. "We also want mom and dad to be here. But they just cannot. They are on your side as well, and they also would love to be here more than anyone." He looked at his feet and did not look at her or Irshita.

"We also miss them. We haven't seen them for seven days. You are not alone. Our birthday is also coming, and I don't think they can come for ours as well." Irshita looked at him and put a hand on his shoulder. He looked up and hugged them.

Renu Kaki called them down. "Akash Baba, come down. The cake is ready."

They went down to complete his birthday celebration. The cake was beautifully made by Renu Kaki, who always acted as a caring aunt in the absence of their parents. He cut the cake. Renu Kaki did her best not to let the children feel the absence of their parents. The children enjoyed the party. Only Akash knew how he wished his parents were there.

Their celebration went on for about eleven in the night. They had games, songs and watched cartoons together. Had snacks and had a lot of cake until he had no place for anything. After the celebra-

tion, he went up to his room and went to bed.
He woke up early in the morning and started to do his studies after breakfast.

His mom and dad had come back the next day in the afternoon to celebrate a late birthday party. They had enjoyed it a lot, and he had not been angry at them for not being there on the day of his birthday. They had taken leave for two days, which was extremely hard in these challenging times. They talked about work, how tough it was and how everyone hardly had any time to sleep.

"Many were just sleeping a couple of hours and not more," his mom said.

They were all busy the whole day, every one of them. He proudly listened to their conversation. He was happy that they were fine. He loved them and respected them even more. After completing his homework, he went to the front yard and talked to his best friend, Arvind. He could not play with him. He only played with his dog, Tommy, the smartest and the best dog he had ever seen. He would throw the ball, and Tommy would bring it. They would play hide and seek. Tommy was extremely good at hiding. He was really smart. Smarter than all the dogs!

The morning turned to evening, the evening turned to night, and night to morning. The same circle went on days after days, everyday, until the birthday of Irshita and Ishani.

His parents had once again taken leave. They had come in the night. The whole family had gathered together. His parents had taken tests before coming home. They always did that to keep him and his sisters safe. The preparations began in the morning. They had called a few family friends as well. Among them was the family of his best friend, Arvind.

The guests arrived in the evening. There were around ten people, and they tried to follow the security protocols as much as possible. But it was a party, so they could not walk around wearing masks. He and Arvind played with Tommy. They played indoor cricket. Tommy enjoyed with them, picking the ball and returning to Akash. After tiring themselves out with cricket, they played with his new play station 4, which his parents had given him for his birthday. He played FIFA and other games that his parents had bought for him. He wished GTA 5 (Grand Theft Auto V) had been among them. Arvind's parents let him play GTA 5. He had got to play it only once, though, with Arvind. He had asked mom and dad for GTA 5, but they said he was too young. But the games that they had brought were not that bad. There was an iron man game where he had to save the world like his parents were doing.

The time passed with lightning speed. In no

time, the night arrived when all the guests left. Akash's parents resumed their medical services. And from the next day, Akash and his twin sisters continued with their routine – online classes, watching TV, playing indoor games and fighting with each other.

Nearly a fortnight passed when suddenly their world began to turn upside-down. It started with a cough. Akash, his sisters and Renu Kaki all got a cough at first, and then it worsened. At first, they thought it was because of all that cold drink, but then they became sick. Too sick. They started to have trouble breathing. His chest ached so much that it felt like there was a steel rode down his spine. His feet hurt when he walked. He could not eat. When he did, he vomited it all out. His sisters and Renu Kaki also complained of similar symptoms.

It felt like every disease in the world had attacked Akash and his family. And he could not do anything. His parents had also returned home. They were also not feeling well. It was a matter of just two days when all of them had to be admitted to the hospital.

Akash was alone in the hospital room. He dreamt that he was walking alone in a dark alley; there was nobody to help him. He did not know where to go. He was confused, and he was scared. He called out the only people who came to his mind:

his mom, dad, Irshita and Ishani. But none of them was around. He was alone. And he felt weak. He was about to walk back where he came from, thinking he may find a way out of this dark. He walked and walked but all in vain. The more he walked, the more tired he felt. He had no one around there to help him. But he did not give up and walked in a straight line. He kept walking until he saw the light far away on the horizon.

"Do not go to the light." He heard a voice. He looked around and, even in the dark, saw his sisters' glowing faces. It made him happy and warm. He looked at his sister, Irshita when someone put a hand on his other shoulder that made him jump. He looked around, and Ishani was standing beside him, smiling at him. Her face was alight in the same way as Irshita's. She laughed at him for jumping at her touch. He made a face and started to laugh as well. Irshita began to laugh with both of them. Their laughter echoed in the empty dark room. He looked at both his sisters and smiled, tears flowing out of his eyes.

"You both will stay with me forever, right?" He asked and looked at their faces. He needed them. Irshita and Ishani, with their glowing faces, knelt in front of him and looked at him, directly into his eyes. He could see their teary eyes.

He remembered the day when they left for the

hostel, just about a year ago. They had to leave the city for college. They had tears in their eyes but managed to control their emotions. They did not let the tears trickle down on their cheeks. Now, on the other hand, they had a smile on their faces with tears in their eyes. Tears they did not hide. They looked more assertive and older – exactly like mom – the same kind and loving eyes, the same loving smile. *They had grown up in such a short time.* He thought and hugged them as tight as he could. Something told him that he would never get that chance again, so he embraced them with all his heart. Tears welled up in his eyes at the thought of their leaving. He did not want them to leave; he desperately held their hands and closed his eyes. And when he opened his eyes, they were gone. He looked towards the light. There was no one.

He opened his eyes with the beeps of the machines all around him. He could not breathe. They had put the mask of the ventilator on his face. He tried with all his might to breathe. He could see doctors standing in the room, worried for him. The nurses ran from one side of the room to the other. A nurse gave him an injection, and soon he closed his eyes.

When Akash opened his eyes at night, he felt much easier breathing. There was a soft light coming from the corridor into his room. Nearly two weeks had passed since the symptoms had first appeared. He was feeling much better. He had not been able to contact his mom and dad. The doctors only told him that they were all recovering and could not speak for another week. So he remained quiet. He was scared. He looked at the light coming inside the room and smiled at the victory he had achieved. To him, all doctors were superheroes. He was a survivor. He took a deep breath, in and out. It hurt a bit, but it was good to know that he could breathe. He took more deep breaths until it did not hurt him to do so.

He closed his eyes again. He still felt sleepy, even though he had slept for a long time. He closed his eyes only to open them to see a doctor and a nurse by his side and a fine streak of the sunlight escaping into the room through the window.

"Good morning Akash, how do you feel?" The doctor smiled at him and felt his chest. "Better?" She asked him to take deep breaths. He did so; it did not hurt him to take deep breaths anymore.

He smiled at the doctor and asked, "How are my sisters?" The doctor avoided the question and looked at the nurse, who looked gravely at him and indicated him not to speak.

He did not say anything, but the doctor's face said otherwise. She left with the nurse to check other patients. The nurse came back to give him

medicines.
"Where are my parents? Are they still recovering?" He asked.

She smiled and said, "They have completely recovered. They are now at home, resting."

"Can I talk to them on the phone?"

"I don't think that would be possible. But I will ask the doctor."

"Thanks." He closed his eyes again when the nurse left.

In the evening, the nurse and the doctor came. First, the doctor checked him thoroughly and then gave the phone to him. "Here it is your parents on phone line."

"Hello?"

His mom's voice was feeble. "How are you?"

"I am better now. The doctor says I am fine. Where is dad?" He heard her crying.

His father came on line and said, "Feeling better, Akash? We will come to see you tomorrow. We are better as well. We will bring you home, if the doctor permits."

The thought of going home gave him a warm feeling. He then remembered his sisters. "How are Irshita and Ishani *didi* and Renu Kaki? I haven't heard about them from anyone."

His father took a deep pause as if trying to control his emotions. "Hospital did not have enough beds, so they were shifted to another hospital."

Akash noticed something strange in his dad's voice. It was shaky yet loud. He remembered his English teacher who had once told him, "People who speak loudly and shout in a discussion are often those people who are living a lie."

His ten-year-old brain screamed; *something is wrong.* "So, it wasn't a dream?" Akash mumbled.

"What?" His dad asked.

Akash remained silent for a few moments.

"Dad, you are lying." And he disconnected the call.

▬

Lonely Footsteps

Early in life, I learned that the truth can be tortuous.

Ten years ago, the truth stared me in the face from the album diary of my mother. And today, once again, it mocks me from this crumpled piece of paper—the disjointed words and shaky handwriting breeding doubt and uncertainty. He is lying on the floor with his head on Granny's lap. He is no more. My father is no more. Just moments ago, I watched him die.

He had come here searching for me, to amend the past. I didn't open the door. I became victim to the past that had seized me for the last ten years and made me what I am today: a "grumpy-faced, frustrated teacher." That's what my students call me behind my back. They do not know how destabilising it is to realise the duplicity of the people whom one trusts.

I had trusted Daddy a lot. I waited for him every Saturday until my worldview was changed when I discovered a letter from my mother.

***

My father would visit me at least one Saturday per month, but I waited for him every Saturday. I would get up early, excited and charged up, climb the only guava tree on the veranda, and eagerly wait for him. The guava tree was my boundary, set by my Granny. She wouldn't let me go beyond that point. She kept an eye on me while I, with my binoculars, would keep a watch on the busy Delhi-Haryana highway, on which trucks and fancy cars would race at super-sonic speed, leaving behind a trail of dust as they tried to outpace each other. I didn't mind inhaling the smoke and dust from the road on Saturdays. The excitement of meeting my father after six days, at times after a fortnight or a month, and listen to his tales of war and heroic experiences was intoxicating.

Every Saturday, I would perch on a branch and wait for him impatiently. In my joy and expectation, I often ate unripe guavas. Granny didn't like my eating of unripe guavas. She would scold me, "You're 12 years old and must learn a bit of womanly etiquette and poise. See all your friends? They look so beautiful, but you? Uff! So unlike your mother. You'll get a stomachache."

Her warnings were inevitably drowned out by the euphoria of my excitement. My heartbeat would increase with each inter-state bus that halted at the bus stop across the road. I would wave my hand the moment I spotted Daddy. As the bus sped away, leaving behind a thick cloud of black fume that enveloped the surroundings, Daddy would frantically wipe the soot from his face. Perched on the guava tree, I would admire his starched soldier's uniform, but when he hugged me, I noticed the food stains on it. "Daddy, you had these vegetable stains last time you visited. Do you have only one uniform?" I would ask innocently.

He would laugh it off, saying, "Can't clean some stains, you know?"

***

One Saturday, I had cautiously balanced myself on the topmost branch of the guava tree, and as I finished my tenth guava, I heard the chime of the wall clock pendulum.

"Granny! What's the time?" I shouted.

"It's 12. Four hours have passed. Come down."

For the first time, I did what she asked. I jumped down, not because she told me to, but because I was tired of hanging onto the thin branch, and my stomach had started hurting.

"What happened?" She came running. "Happy? Now let me see. Have you hurt yourself?"

She began to dust off my favourite blue dress, but her eyes looked beyond me.

"Why don't you sit here on the veranda and wait for him?"

I ran inside without answering her, concealing my disappointment. Turning my back to her, I unzipped my school bag, kept on the bed, and swallowed some medicine for stomachache.

"What are you eating?"

I quickly put the bag back. "Nothing."

I hadn't heard her come in.

"When will you understand, my girl, that your father will come when he feels like coming and not because-" she stopped.

I gave her a stern look and drank a glass of water. After a pause, she said, "For him, you're just a responsibility, forced upon him by those self-appointed guardians of the law. Understand?"

I did not comprehend what she was trying to convey. I only knew that my father loved me enough to take leave from his office and visit on Saturdays at least once a month.

"There he is." She saw him entering the house.

I ran to him.

Later, when I approached him with Granny's

doubts, he was not angry but brushed it off, saying, "The office keeps me busy, Roohi. It's not so easy to be a soldier in the army. Do you understand that?"

Even as he said this, he was looking beyond me at the only photograph of my mother decorating the wall, surrounded by dark, dust-laden threads of dirt. Though his voice sounded feeble, it dispelled my fears. I looked at Granny, who was sitting at a distance and chopping vegetables. I smiled at her triumphantly and hopped on Daddy's back.

"This is your punishment, Daddy. Now give me a piggyback ride!"

He let out a delighted laugh and carried me to the front lawn.

***

It was as though our lives had gotten stuck, like a needle on a 78 rpm record. As soon as we were alone, Granny would marshal her fears and puncture my happiness.

"He is lying. He's telling a lie. He's not in the army anymore. He had to leave after the war. Understand?"

I would hate her for being so dismissive of my father. "Do you understand what I'm saying? A few self-proclaimed keepers of morality and law ordered him to become your guardian. Understand this and understand it now, my little girl."

The desperation in her voice would make me growl like a wounded cat,

"You make me feel so unwanted, so-"

Her choked voice would melt my heart. Despite our disagreements about Daddy, I would never leave the hateful venom to seep through our skin and become septic. She was the only one I had and was too precious to me!

"Oh, my dear Granny, you're so dramatic! My God, you've put on weight. See, I can't even lock my fingers around your waist now."

"Naughty. In school, if any student of mine played pranks with me, I would deduct five marks, but with you, I am so helpless."

***

I missed Daddy and his war stories. Whenever he narrated his experiences at the war front, it accelerated my heartbeat.

"And Roohi, you know that night I couldn't sleep - the fierce sound of the bombardments, gunshots - and in all that mad cacophony, I saw a child crossing our boundary, crying. I followed him, crossed the border unknowingly and next-"

He would describe incidents so vividly that at

night I would shiver in my dreams - fierce artillery sound, wounded soldiers, and a swarm of people appearing from nowhere with a question on their faces: now where? I used to hear innocent shrieks and screams of unknown, frightened faces. The images haunted me even during the day. I would cry and curse the people who began the war. Even as a child, I thought that all battles, riots, and acts of terrorism were barbaric. I hated violence. I hated killing.

To me, my father was a hero, a brave soldier, but Granny never believed his anecdotes. She would dismiss his anecdotes as, "A figment of imagination."

"Why, Granny?"

"You wouldn't understand. Go and play with your friends," she would reply.

"But I don't have any friends, Granny." I would reveal my lonely heart, but she never recognized this truth. She always thought I was making an excuse. "People think that I am the cause of my mother's death. They call me 'a curse' and jeer at me. Why, Granny? Why does everyone call me 'a curse'?"

She never answered my question but would suddenly be limping across the room to the kitchen, moaning, "It's so painful, this arthritis will kill me." She avoided such delicate confrontations and would go, leaving me to be my playmate.

But not my Daddy.

"They're foolish. You're precious, my little angel, and that's the truth," he would say loud enough for Granny to hear and immediately take me into a world of love and understanding.

He would tell me stories about him and my mother.

"She was so beautiful that the moment I saw her, I fell in love with her. We were soulmates. I could understand her mind, even before she put her thoughts into words."

As he unfolded the layers of my mother's life, I would become utterly mesmerized.

"After we were married, we went to Agra to see the Taj Mahal. She was seeing it for the first time. You know the Taj Mahal? The monument built by the Mughal Emperor in memory of his beloved wife. Did you read about it in your history books?"

"Yes, King Shahjahan-"

"That's right."

He would tell me about the various places that he and my mother visited and their long histories. I swelled with pride at his knowledge while Granny looked at him with disbelief.

Despite her condescension, I enjoyed his stories, all full of bravery and humanity. With him, I forgot that no one played with me, and everyone considered me a 'curse.' He helped me overcome my fear of darkness. With him, I learned to be confident. He was my world. I trusted my father and believed him when he hesitatingly told me that he could not take me where he lived because his work required him to travel a lot.

"But all children stay with their parents."

"Yes, but we're unique," he thoughtfully replied.

I believed him.

***

"He will not come. It's getting dark now. Go and study," Granny said that night after seeing me sitting with a morose face, still waiting for my father. Her words pierced my heart.

Tired and bored, I snuck to the rooftop alone. My eyes scanned through the stars in the frozen sky and found the brightest one. It was a game that I played too often. For me, the star that shone the most was my mother. I shared my innermost thoughts with her, my star-mother – dreams that I could not communicate with anybody else, not even with Granny.

"Why did you leave me, Ma? Nobody plays with me. Why is Granny so against Daddy? I don't like it. You must do something."

Alone, gazing at the night's sky, I entered into a secret world of my creation. I saw my mother in a red *saree*, smiling at my father, exchanging garlands; I saw her playing with me; I saw myself playing with the children downstairs; I saw my mother singing a lullaby to me; I saw her putting me to bed and whispering, "Be brave."

"Roohi, what are you doing upstairs so late? Come down; it's raining." Granny's voice slashed through my imaginary world. I looked around. I was drenched and alone.

"Coming."

I ran towards the staircase, but my foot got entangled in a loose wire. I cried out.

"What happened?" I heard Granny's shaky voice.

The echo in her voice made me feel as if somebody was calling me from a distance. I desperately tried to save myself from tumbling down, but it was as though somebody was pushing me to see the world upside down. With my back curved, my right hand banged against the wooden box kept in the corner of the rickety stairs. It rolled down along with me, and files, notebooks, photographs, and loose, yellowish, dust-laden papers flew out of it and surrounded me. My heart pounded, and my head swirled. I rolled down. Breathless and panting vigorously, I regained my senses only at the last step of the staircase. When I looked up, Granny's petrified face greeted me. She stared at me and the floor, scattered with papers and photographs I had never seen. Slowly, I got up to examine the various parts of my body. Relieved that I could walk, I gave a meek smile to Granny.

"Oh, my God," she cried.

"I'm fine, Granny." I had to pretend to soothe her racing heart. But her eyes were looking over me at the deluge of papers, a diary and an album. She hurriedly began to pick up the moth-eaten photographs.

"No, don't touch. I'll do it," she said, covering the photographs with her heavy body.

"What is it, Granny?"

There was a disquieting flutter in the air.

“No, I mean, go and put some ointment on those scratches, my child.”

“Don’t worry,” I replied and picked up a photograph. Granny’s eyes were on me. Helplessly, she squatted on the floor.

“What’s this Granny, and who is this man in the photograph? And why is he putting turban and so nicely dressed up?”

She didn't reply. She didn’t even look at me or the photograph.

“Granny?”

I was puzzled. I looked at Granny and then at the photograph. She kept sitting, staring beyond me. Her gaze frightened me. I picked up the album and began to leaf through it. It held my mother’s wedding photos.

“Why have you kept this in a box? It’s so pretty, Granny! Daddy looks so handsome.”

Silence.

I turned another page. It was blank.

Then another.

Then another. Again, a blank page stared at me.

I looked at her questioningly. She still refused to look at me. I turned the next page and on it was a small note at the bottom of the page: *He has been missing for the last five years. We do not know whether he is alive or dead. People tell me he is dead. Should I believe it?* It was my mother's handwriting.

Granny was still in a trance. Sitting next to her, I turned another page, and four words, written in capital letters, stared back at me: *MY SECOND LIFE BEGINS.* Accompanying that page were photographs. Hesitantly, I took a photo out of the album and saw my mother marrying another man I had never seen.

"Who's he?"

No response.

"Granny."

I shook her to bring her out of her trance. Her hands were cold, and her eyes vacant.

"Granny, who is he?"

"Your father," she whispered.

I couldn't say anything.

"She married him. We thought..."

But I couldn't listen to her. I picked up the little diary and turned the first page.

"I'm at a crossroad. Arun Pandey, my first husband, has returned after six years. I waited for him for five years and believed what people told me when he did not return. They told me that he had become a martyr at the battlefront. I trusted them. And then, like a breath of fresh air, Sudhir entered into my life. My heart was pining for attention, my young body ached for a gentle touch, and my ears were longing to hear flattering whispers. I recklessly fell in love with Sudhir. I remarried, despite village elders raising a few concerns about his caste. But when have matters of the heart bowed to prudence?

Now, Arun has returned and is asserting his conjugal rights after six years. What should I do? The village elders are on his side. They're asking me to return to Arun. The village Panchayat, who is supposed to be the most knowledgeable about law, legality and morality (really?), has declared my second marriage to Sudhir Ram 'illegal.' This means the child I'm carrying is illegitimate, and me a.... Do women not have the freedom to make a choice? Do I not have a heart?"

I turned another page.

"I'm tired. Baba is silent. Ma keeps crying. The villagers are putting pressure on them. They say it's a matter of 'village honour.' After all, I didn't get their blessings to marry Sudhir, a Dalit. But what should I do now?"

The pages were blank after this. Dumbfounded, I kept sitting next to Granny. I could not comprehend the weight of what my mother had written, but I understood the importance of blank pages.

A deathlike silence suffused our tiny home. We both sat on the floor for hours. And we would have kept sitting like statues until dawn had there been no knock at the door. From the urgency of the knock, I recognised the person. I did not get up or run to open the door. Granny did.

For the first time in my 12 years, I wished Daddy had not come.

He entered the room and tried to greet me, but I could not return his easiness.

"Aha, here you are! My little angel is annoyed with me. I can see that. I'm sorry, but I was working, Roohiii," he said, sitting beside me and stressing the last syllable of my name. "It was just one of those bad days. Anyway, see what I got for you."

He removed the perfumed decorations from a

chocolate box, took out my favourite chocolate, and brought it near my lips.

"For my little angel."

I shoved his hand away. He gave me a puzzled look.

"What happened? Is something wrong?" he asked Granny.

She had already turned her face away, hiding her moist eyes.

"Roohi, what is it?" His anxious voice pierced my heart.

I gave him the diary.

He left without saying a word.

***

After this, Daddy stopped coming. Soon, Granny and I left our home and moved to Bhimtaal, a serene, mountainous area situated in Uttarakhand. We rented a small apartment near a lake. In the evenings, I sat on the shore, searching "truth" in the stillness of the water. Is truth merely what we believe and want to be, or is it the reality that we fail to see?

With time, the list of unanswered questions only increased. Was Daddy spoiling me to redeem himself? Did he love me, or was everything just a formality? Was it penance to do away with the guilt of not giving my mother a chance to live? Why do women always have to suffer? Even our mythological women characters — from Damayanti to Draupadi to Sita — had to suffer. Why? These questions turned my life into a battlefield of unresolved complexes and dead hopes for the next ten years.

Unable to sleep one night, I wandered through the dark, narrow alleys of my childhood memories. I spent hours in contemplation until a loud thumping on the door broke the solemnity of my thoughts.

Frightened, I tiptoed to the door. Accompanying the banging was a faint voice that seemed familiar.

"Who is it?" Granny's sleepy voice interrupted my concentration.

I tried looking through the frosted glass, straining my eyes in the thick December fog outside. I heard footsteps pacing from the window to the door. It had an eerie effect of loneliness.

"A man in an overcoat? Who could be at this hour?" I tried wiping the frost from the glass. His back was towards me. I saw him bend down with one hand on his stomach, recoiling. He gave a feeble tap on the door again. “Roohiii!”

“Daddy!” the word involuntarily escaped my mouth.

What are you doing, Roohi? my inner voice immediately imprisoned me. I could not move. My legs froze.

There was then a violent, hurried thumping. I looked out again. “Oh, my God!” He was lying on the floor. I ran out, disregarding the protests of my inner voice. Granny joined me. “What happened, Roohi?”

“It’s Daddy!” I flung open the door. “Daddy! What happened? Open your eyes, Daddy!” I cried. “Daddy!”

He blinked. Granny limped inside and brought a glass of water. She squatted on the floor and quickly Daddy’s head from the floor onto her lap and wiped the thin line of blood vomit from the corners of his mouth with her *saree* corner.

“I am sorry, Roohi. See, now along with vegetable stains, my shirt has bloodstains too,” he mumbled, giving a weak smile through his obvious pain.

“Shh, don’t speak, Daddy. Hold on. I’ll call the doctor. Keep your eyes open.”

But his arms fell listlessly to his sides.

"Roohi... it's no use," he could barely utter. I stared back at him. I looked at his arms, frozen on the ground, and his left fist tightly closed around a white paper peeking out from between his bony fingers. I used all my strength to open his hand and pull out the crumpled paper.

"Dear Roohi,
I don't have time. I know you're annoyed with me. Before dying, I want to apologise and make a confession."

My heartbeat increased, fingers trembled, and throat ached with dryness. I looked at Daddy's face, lips laced with blood, and then at the paper in my hand. The very next moment, I lost him. Forever.

"Dear Roohi,

I know you're annoyed with me. Before dying, I want to apologise and make a confession. I'm a liar. Whatever stories I told you about the war were untrue. Whatever I told you about your mother and myself was untrue. The only truth that I told you was that I loved your mother too much. We were together only for two months, and then the war broke out, and I had to report at the battle line. You will never be able to comprehend how I missed her at the war front. I was fighting at the battlefront, but my thoughts were with her. I wanted to be with her. I loved her more than my life. And love, you know, can make people do foolish things. Now that you're grown up, I'm sure you'll understand this human weakness. After all, isn't it said that everything is fair in love and war? But the gruesome mistake that I committed was that I forgot love does not exist in still waters. It's a deep flowing river, and people have to swim along together, willingly. I forgot that one could not force love, but then neither can it be withheld. Isn't that right?

To be honest, my vision was foggy then. The timing was wrong. After seeing the worst side of human life during the war and then as a prisoner of war, I had lost sanity. After returning, which I thought was nothing less than a miracle, I just wanted to celebrate life, love, and be with your mother, my wife. She was my world.

I was an orphan, and you know that, right? No, no, don't get me wrong. I am not justifying my actions.

Now, at the last stage of my illness, I'll not tell a lie. Yes, I was responsible for your parents' death to some extent, but I didn't kill them. I only found their bodies hanging from a tree. Whether they were killed or committed suicide, I don't know. She married outside her caste, a Dalit, and you know how village elders and Panchayat are so against such a union. You must have read about the Hathras incident recently – how a 19-year-old Dalit girl was gang-raped and left in the fields to die. This case refreshed the memories of your mother and biological father, a Dalit. It took me back nearly 25 years ago.

Roohi, I couldn't sleep after reading about this incident. It pricked, hurt and broke me. Twenty-five years earlier, it happened with your mother and now again! Let me honestly confess, Roohi; I was not responsible for what happened to your parents. Yes, to appease my bruised ego, I took the help of the village elders and the Panchayat. For them, it became a matter of dignity and honour. And by the time I realised the politics of the caste, religion and the Panchayat, it was too late! Society, you see, makes it very difficult for women to have a voice and choice. It's a toxic, patriarchal world. To this day, it stifles me to remember that night. Your parents ran away, hid in the lavatory of a railway station, a few youths, five of them, dragged your mother and father to the nearby fields. It was dark and isolated. Your mother begged for her life, reminded them she had just given birth to a baby. But when has hatred acquiesced to pleadings?

I tried to save them but couldn't. I was one, and they were many. I ran nearly two kilometres to call the police. There was a threatening silence by the time I returned – only two half-naked bodies were hanging from a tree.

I left the place, taking with me the wails of your Granny and Grandfather, who couldn't save their only daughter. It was far worse than the wars that nations fight. Was it a case of an Honour killing? I don't know, but I never wanted her to die, Roohi. And this is the truth, nothing but the truth, my love!

One thing more. For the last ten years, I haven't been able to sleep peacefully. The moment I shut my eyes, your wounded expression and questioning eyes haunt me. I know you think I am guilty. I should have told you all this long ago, but I just couldn't muster the strength to face you. And now, on my deathbed, I want to clear all your doubts and unanswered questions.

The truth, my little angel, is that when I came to meet you on Saturdays, it was not because of guilt or to redeem myself or to do penance, but because I loved you. When I met you on Saturdays, it was not because the Panchayat ordered me to do so but because you had become my lifeline. When I came there on Saturdays, it was because I considered you my first daughter. I loved you and still do. So what if I am not your biological father? You're the daughter of my first wife, whom I loved more than my life. And yes, I was a coward not to accept you publicly.

This is the truth of my life. The only truth.

Just remember that I love you and always have loved you.

Remember this.

Always.

Your loving,

Daddy.

***

A scream escaped my throat. I kept looking at the crinkled paper in my palm, and an avalanche of tears streamed down my cheeks. I looked at the sky, at the face resting peacefully on Granny's lap, and heard the inaudible sound of lonely footsteps going further away.

▬

My Father

A month's winter vacation had brought me to the small two-room house of my parents in Hathras, Uttar Pradesh. I had not been allowed to visit this place, though it is only 181 kilometres away from Delhi. Every year, during the holidays, my mother came to Delhi, where I lived with my maternal uncle. But this year, I had insisted on visiting Hathras, despite my uncle's reluctance.

"Uncle, I want to see my father." I'd not seen him for the last eight years.

"But your father is not well, darling, and your mother would be angry."

"I don't care. All my friends ask me about Baba and our *hing* (asafoetida) farming."

"So, what? You're not a child. In a few months, you will enter college."

I refused to listen to him and forced him to take an oath that he would not tell Ma.

I knew Baba was not well. When I was eight years old, I was dispatched to my uncle's place stealthily. No questions asked.

Much later, Uncle told me that Baba was suffering from a dreadful illness and that my mother had to look after him and teach in a local school and monitor the agricultural fields. I don't remember much of him, except that he worked on his agricultural land for long hours, played with me, read stories, and drew a boundary line, *Laksham Rekha,* which Shanti Bua (aunt), his sister, and I were not permitted to cross. And then, one evening, a big crowd gathered in front of the gate and surrounded Baba. I could only hear the indistinct cacophony of voices. And the next moment, I saw him running in a chaotic state, screaming, "Shanti . . . Shanti!"

Ma began to tremble. She held me tightly and called up Uncle.

"Where is aunt?" I asked.

Ma didn't reply. The next morning, I remember waking up at Uncle's home. And since then, I have been living with him.

***

I entered the already half-open front door with a mind full of ideas and a heart full of smiles. There was no one around. I tip-toed a bit further and suddenly felt cold water below my feet as if awakening me to an unknown reality. I looked down and barely managed to escape falling.

"Ma! What's this?" I shouted.

"Oh, don't worry. . . I just thought the place needed cleaning up." I recognised the voice.

"Baba!"

I was finally seeing him after so many years. He had grown old. With a spring in my step, I rushed at him.

"Shanti . . . seeing you after so many days . . . where did you go?" The cold, emotionless texture of the voice ruptured my excitement.

"No, Baba, it's me, your sweetie pie, Rachna," I corrected him.

Unmindful of the flooded space and my presence, he continued eating a banana. There was no whirl of excitement at seeing his daughter after so many years.

I blinked.

A rope of unpredictable fear suddenly seemed to tighten around my neck!

I kept looking at his stony eyes and distorted facial twitch. Suddenly he brought his face nearer to me and whispered: "You know, Deepa is trying to kill me?"

The juices in my stomach stopped churning. He spoke in a voice like the turbulent, painful music of a sandstorm, enveloping a vacant room. He was reeking of tobacco. I rummaged through my childhood memories. Baba never used to smoke; he hated it.

"Something is wrong?" I muttered, hardly audible.

Trembling all over, I hit the glass table. The sweet lemon water flowed all over the dining table. I stared into Baba's hollow, dilated eyes and waited for the horrid joke to reach its climax, expecting the room to reverberate with his laughter and his arms to envelop me in a tight hug.

But no, unaffected by my expectations and fear, Baba carried on with his rancour and accusations.

"You know, she hired goons to do the task. They were here just now. I heard their footsteps last night, too."

Baba's monologues appeared volcanically coloured, only to turn to grey ashes. "He was in a black overcoat, a hat, and had a pipe between his lips. He was here last evening, staring at me." His description reminded me of the times when he had read Sherlock Holmes stories to me. "You know," he whispered, "she always wanted to kill me."

Stunned, I stood there, frozen.

The pages from my childhood diary seemed to have been swiftly wiped away by the turbulent tidal wave of time.

He was blabbering and pacing abruptly around the table. My hands grew cold, and I began to sweat profusely. I couldn't make any sense of the situation, and in my mind, there ensued a battle between expectations and shock.

The Montblanc fountain pen that I'd bought with my pocket money for Baba slipped from my hands. My childhood memory had prompted me to buy it as Baba loved writing with fountain pens only. For a moment, I kept watching it as it floated in the stagnant water at my feet, wondering its purpose. Quietly, I picked it back up, stuffed the pen along with my priceless memories back in the laptop bag, and carefully cushioned myself between the soft pillows on the settee, impatiently waiting for Ma.

"Are you listening, Shanti?" He jumped on the settee and sat next to me. I clutched at the cushion and put it next to my face, not knowing what his next actions would be.

I meekly replied, “Yes, Baba.”

“Yesterday, they tried pushing me into the water, but I pushed them! Poor guys! That’s why I flooded the house today, to clean it!” His lips stretched in a queer smile.

My heart somersaulted rapidly into my throat, my mouth, my head. I half-closed my eyes, expecting something worse to happen.

“Ma!” I screamed as soon as I saw her opening the front door and ran towards her.

“Rachna! Why have you come? I told you I’d be there day after tomorrow.”

A bombshell. My face fell.

I had thought of giving Ma and Baba a surprise but never expected that the Universe had something equally shocking in store for me.

“No, no, don’t misunderstand, Rachna. I’m just a little surprised. I was planning to come to Delhi in two days,” she quickly amended her statement and hugged me. There was a helper behind her. She asked him to clean the house and take Baba inside.

“Where were you? What happened? Why are there so many medicines?” I asked.

"It's okay. I'll tell you later." I saw Baba recoiling in a corner. Ma rushed inside.

With unanswered questions and a sinking fear, I felt like an unarmed creature, writhing in pain, caught in an unexpected blitzkrieg.

Jubilation got lost in the din of despair.

That night, Ma came to my room, tired, looking much older and worn out. She hugged me tightly, wept, but did not tell me anything.

I had understood, though.

"Ma!"

"Hmmm?"

"Ma, I was wondering." My throat was dry. Words were getting lost in the turmoil of emotions. "Maaaa!"

"Will you say something? Forget it, tell me about your school. How is your friend Neha?"

My mind was racing on a different path.

"Ma, why don't you come to Delhi and stay with me? Let's admit Baba to an institute."

"Shut up," she said, cutting me short.

"But why, Ma?"

"You will not understand. Do you see all these medals? These are his. He was brilliant. He studied on scholarship throughout his life. He was a gold medalist. I always borrowed his notes." A smile spread on her lips, and her eyes sparkled even in the darkness as she remembered 'those' days.

"Then what happened?"

She ignored my question and continued with her precious memories. "He was following in the footsteps of Norman Borlaug, the great agricultural scientist, you know. That's why he returned to his roots, leaving a respectable scientific research job. He wanted to experiment on his ancestral agricultural field. He didn't force me to leave the job. I loved your father so much that nothing else mattered more than his company."

I knew then that she would not give up on him.

"But Ma, now? What about your life, my life, our lives? Listen Ma, let's all stay together in Delhi—Baba, you, and me. And in Delhi, I'll be there to help you take care of Baba."

"No. Your Baba always wanted to return to his

roots."

"What roots are you talking about, Ma?" I was determined not to give up so soon. "He doesn't remember anything, now. He doesn't even recognise me. And . . . and . . . I don't think God wants us to suffer needlessly, especially when Baba isn't even aware of his surroundings."

She remained silent. She seemed to have accepted her fate. And any revolt against a destiny she could not change appeared pointless to her. "I'll never disrespect or go against his wishes. And Rachna, he was not like this before your aunt's death. You don't remember when he was not like this." I could hear the pain in her voice.

***

Yes, Ma, I don't remember Baba when he was not like this!

I only have a faint memory of him playing with me, taking me out on long walks, teaching me to dream big, reading stories of real heroes. He never liked reading fairy tales to me.

Yes, Ma, you're right; I don't remember when he was not like this!

I was sitting on the veranda, and Baba was sitting across from me. He was staring at the walls—not speaking, not listening, just staring beyond the walls, absorbed in his private world.

So, who was my Baba? The father who I remember or the person sitting across, lost in his private world? Or . . .

"Shanti . . . where have you been all these years? I was so worried?"

Or this man who doesn't recognise his daughter; only remembers his sister, Shanti.

"Don't you mind, Baby. He only remembers his sister. He was very attached to her," Ramu Kaka, who had been sweeping the floor, explained to me apologetically.

I was in no mood to engage with him. I was engrossed in examining my life through the wide-angle lens of memories, and memories are often lethal and self-absorbing. They cut across time and sentiments.

I was merely trying to understand Baba, his past, and our future.

***

Often, late at night, he screamed. "They are coming . . . they are coming . . . they killed her!"

Whenever he shouted in fear, Ma would give him some medicines and sit beside him, caressing his forehead.

He saw shadows, had delusions and hallucinations, and we were unable to clear his foggy vision. Our dinners were punctuated with violent protests, tempers, and smouldering hatred. Often, he erupted into bouts of unpredictable rage on not getting the things he demanded, and he was always scolding us incoherently.

We could only watch helplessly.

Though, just a few days into my winter holidays, I'd gotten used to his oddities. However, the lurking fear of the unpredictability of Baba's eccentricities was disconcerting. And very soon, my fear turned into a paralytic experience.

It was early in the morning, and I'd just returned after dropping Ma off at school. I was happy. Ma had given me her consent to pursue my dream —the course in textile designing. But the moment I pushed the front door open, my excitement turned into a nightmare.

There he was, my Baba, hurriedly pacing around the room and in equally rapid speed repeating in a loop some scientific formula. He was playing the role of several agricultural scientists. His jangled repetitions, bouncing off the room's walls, pierced my happiness with needle-like shrillness. I asked him if he wanted something. There was a sudden mood change. He looked at me as if I'd destroyed his meditation.

A tense silence followed.

I decided to exit from his radar peacefully, and while going to the other room, I noticed him squatting on the floor, his eyes begging for help. I ran back to him. He was breathing heavily.

"Seizure?" My heart began to race, and I immediately pressed Ma's telephone number.

"Ma . . . come . . ." I could hardly get the words out.

She didn't ask anymore. As I disconnected the telephone call, I heard a hurried bang. The ground slipped from beneath my feet.

I froze.

There he was, lying on the floor, shaking violently, sweating, his clothing soiled in faeces.

Terrified, instead of running towards him, I ran away from him to the other room, bolted the door, and waited for Ma and Ramu Kaka to arrive. I began to pray for some miracle to happen, for years to roll back, for life to run backwards, and for the present to be deleted entirely. I begged and prayed and bribed the unseen Power with innumerable gifts until Ma returned.

"Ma, what happened to Baba?" I asked her with tears streaming down my face. She hugged me. This time she didn't avoid answering me. She took me to the hospital with her.

I heard the word for the first time in the hospital. The 13-letter word that changed the course of our lives.

Schizophrenia.

No sooner did we return than I jumped on my laptop. I googled the word that I had just heard. "Why me? How could it happen to Baba? Is it in our genes? Will I also become like this? Is it hereditary?" Innumerable questions invaded my peace.

That night I couldn't sleep.

Schizophrenia no longer remained just a word. It was the word that changed my world. It took Baba away from me. Had I not seen its physical manifestation at home, I might have giggled at the word 'schizophrenia,' assuming it to be some weird plant specimen. It was all so surreal as if we were the characters in some horror film. I just waited for the bubble to burst, for the nightmare to end.

But Alas! Every morning I woke up to relive the same nightmare, day after day. I wanted to return to Uncle, where there was peace. But, what about Ma?

I realized Baba had 'gone.'

He had gone far away from my life, our lives.

***

"Ma, why does Baba always take Shanti aunt's name? He just remembers her. Not me. Why, Ma?" I had to ask this question that was troubling me from the day I arrived here.

This time Ma did not avoid my question.

"Shanti was burned alive."

"What?"

"Yes, she was burned alive. I think you are grown up enough now to understand what I'm about to tell you."

My mouth went dry. Ma remained silent.

"Then tell."

“I’m sorry.” She looked up at the sky. “Shanti was raped and burned by upper castes’ men. Your Baba couldn’t save her. He was forced, threatened to watch the brutal violation of his sister’s body. She was then burned alive. It made him drift on the edges of life . . . of sanity, Rachna.” Ma began to cry. She couldn’t speak further.

“And the police?”

She nodded, “Nothing . . . no complaint. Ours was a weak voice.”

“Meaning?”

“Oh, child. Your Baba is a Dalit. Your aunt was a Dalit.”

“But what is a Dalit? Are they not human?”

“I don’t know.”

“And you?”

Just at that moment, Baba yelled. She left me without answering my query.

Was I looking at life through a small hole?

I again took the help of Mr Google. The Wikipedia definition was simple—*Dalit is a term used for people belonging to castes in India who have been sub-*

jected to untouchability. In the footnotes was an article from an online publication that annihilated my spirit.

> *"Khairlanji massacre—In 2006, in Khairlanji in Maharashtra, members of a Dalit family were tortured and beaten to death by men of the dominant Kunbi and Kalar caste. This was because the Dalit (Bhotmange) family was prosperous and had previously helped a Dalit man escape the violence that upper-caste men perpetrated. To teach them a lesson, the mother, her daughter, and her two sons were dragged out of their house. The four were stripped and paraded naked. One of the sons was asked to have sex with his sister and was beaten to death when he refused. The perpetrators mutilated their private parts, gang-raped the women. According to some reports, the men continued to rape their dead bodies long after they had died. . . ." (Livewire-The Wire - 30 September 2020)*

I couldn't read any further and rushed to the washroom.

When I came out of the washroom, Ma stood at the door with my cell phone, reading the text.

I threw myself into her arms.

"Is this the reason why Uncle has given me his surname and not that of Baba's?" I asked feebly.

Ma didn't answer.

I felt a droplet fall onto my cheek.

***

I began to live in constant fear, fear of the unknown, fear of belonging to a caste considered to be in the lowest rung of the caste system. But then, didn't Mahatma Gandhi fight against this segregation? I pondered. I regretted my decision to visit my ancestral hometown.

Sometimes living in ignorance is bliss!

I was observing Baba sitting opposite me on a reclining chair. He looked at me. Looking at him, I wondered if anyone can say today that he was a topper, a genius, and a gold medalist.

"Baba, why do we have to carry our history with us?" I questioned, knowing that there would be no answer.

He kept looking at me. A lingering sense of hopelessness had encompassed me. I looked at the open sky in anger at the injustice of the Universe. Suddenly Baba groaned. His face began to contort, he threw away the Rubik's Cube that he was holding in his hands, and his legs began to bend.

I screamed, "Ramu Kaka!"

Kaka came running and immediately held him tightly from behind. Baba was unrecognizable. I kept watching him. He was blabbering, stomping his feet, and pushing Kaka away violently. He reminded me of several homeless destitute, who I often see at the traffic lights in Delhi. Baba was sick—very sick.

"Baby . . . medicine . . . pink capsule," Kaka told me to get it from the bedside table. After a few minutes, the situation was under control. Baba had no memory of what had happened to him a few moments ago.

"Ramu, get my Rubik's Cube. Who threw it there?" Baba asked, annoyed.

Ramu Kaka gave him the toy and busied himself in his chores.

An overwhelming sense of defeat overpowered me as I began to wait for Ma's return.

What is Schizophrenia? What kind of a shattered world is he living in? Will things ever be the same again? What next? Why us? Who am I? Daughter of an awarded agricultural scientist? Or of a madman? How does Ma feel? Is this love, or fear of the unknown? Or only pity? Or is she living in the pit of memories—memories frozen in time?

Several questions began to invade my existence. I was throwing questions into a dark tunnel, waiting for answers. No ray of hope seemed to be greeting me at the end of the tunnel. I decided to wrestle my adversaries alone. I decided to script our lives differently, with my own newfound rules not mentioned in any rule book of life. I chose not to get stuck in a time-warp and get crushed. I internalized the grief and let out a wild scream – a scream to celebrate freedom from self-abnegation.

"What happened? Why are you screaming?" Ma asked, holding me tightly around the shoulders.

I smiled. "Nothing."

"But I heard you screaming."

I paused, looked at her intensely, made her sit beside me. She drew in her breath anxiously.

"Ma, we're all going to Delhi."

She kept looking at me, surprised at my commanding tone.

"Ma . . . are you listening?"

"Yes . . . but I have told you."

"I'm not asking you. We are going, or else . . . I'm going to come here to live."

"Rachna!"

"No, I'm not listening. You can shout, slap, bully me . . . do whatever . . . but I'm Dr Suresh Ram's daughter . . . and I'm stubborn like him. He brought you here, but now he is sick and needs a better medical facility. So, no questions asked. We're going, Ma. We're not going to live in this valley of fear. Period."

She was surprised at the finality in my tone.

Silence, impregnated with the buoyancy of an unknown but hopeful world! It was like burning camphor, extinguishing the ghost and shadows of the past in its fragrance.

> "Ma, I refuse to be the victim and would not let you also be the victim of history, time, and circumstances. I'll get him back on track. The medical science has advanced. Psychiatry has advanced. I have found my mission. Henceforth, I'll be his caregiver. And you wait and see." Inadvertently, tears began to slip down my cheeks. "Baba would be fine, soon."

"Hey Shanti, why are you crying?" Baba said, wiping my tears. He had been observing me. "Don't cry . . . look at me! I'm not frightened. I know those people are trying to murder me . . . I'm the only witness to their crimes . . . destroy everything on my computer. Everything . . . hard disk . . . destroy it . . . Shanti."

I had missed his touch. For this little happiness, I didn't object to his delusion.

"She is not Shanti . . . she is your . . ." Ma intercepted.

"Don't, Ma. Let him live in his world . . . if that gives him happiness. What is, *is.* But he will not be like this for long. That I promise you, Ma."

Ma smiled. There was a sense of relief on her face, seeing my determination. She understood that she was no more alone.

I took a deep breath. Ma hugged me tightly.

The aroma of a new beginning was intoxicating.

▬

About the Author

Geeta L Sahai is an author, awarded filmmaker and a mental health campaigner. After working as a journalist for several years, she is a full-time writer-filmmaker now. She writes fiction and non-fiction. Her work has been published by HarperCollins, Mithra Publishing and Niyogi Books.

Her fiction is inspired by real-life stories. Her meticulous research enriches her work with evocative themes and unforgettable characters.

Her film—*I Remember...* won many national and international awards (streaming on Disney-Hotstar.) She is actively involved in mental health advocacy. She is a recipient of the REX-Karmaveer-Bronze and Silver Karmaveer-Chakra Award (instituted by iCONGO - International-Confederation-of-NGO - in partnership with the UN) 2014 and 2019, respectively.

Once is Not Enough is her second collection of short stories.

She lives in Delhi-NCR, India.

June 2021

Email: geeta@geetalalsahai.com

Social media links:

Website: https://geetalalsahai.com

Author page on Amazon:
https://www.amazon.in/Geeta-Sahai/e/B01HOXWA7G/ref=ntt_dp_epwbk_0

Author page on Goodreads: https://www.goodreads.com/author/show/21179571.Geeta_Lal_Sahai

Facebook:

https://www.facebook.com/Authorfilmmakergeeta

Twitter:

https://twitter.com/GeetaSahai

Instagram:

https://www.instagram.com/geetasahai

Linkedin:

https://www.linkedin.com/in/geeta-sahai-0921976/

Thank You

To an author, nothing is more precious than receiving readers'

feedback.

I would be highly grateful if you could leave the review of this book on the Book Review page – the same link and page from where you bought the book.

Reviews by readers matter immensely to authors. It will take hardly a minute but will surely help me to reach out to many more readers.

A very big Thank You in advance.

I impatiently look forward to receiving your feedback.

You can always drop an email and visit my website to be the first to hear about my NEW releases and subscribe to my mailing list. I promise I will not spam you and will only contact you when my new release is to happen.

Website: https://geetalalsahai.com
Email: geeta@geetalalsahai.com

THANK YOU.

Books By This Author

Beyond Music: Maestros In Conversation

"This book offers a rare window into the lives and struggles of maestros. The volume, befitting multiple sequels, is valuable in terms of its archival potential since some of the grand maestros are no longer with us." (Music critic- KALYANEE RAJAN)

The book has 25 priceless interviews of Hindustani Classical Music Maestros. Beyond Music - is not just about music; it is an exciting journey into the minds of the musicians, bringing alive the fragrance of their musical thinking.

When Goodbye Begins: Life Takes Over

“Powerful, heartbreaking...Remarkable” (Amazon Reviewer).

Hope allows us to move ahead even if the truth is distorted. In this collection of five stories memories and grief play a crucial part. Inspired by real-life incidents, these five stories portray the fragility of the human mind.

Printed in Great Britain
by Amazon